To Tom, Sarah,
Nigel, Sabrina and Kim
for their kind help
and advice

Mummy Laid an Egg!

by
Babette Cole

Jonathan Cape

London

"Right," said mum and dad.
"We think it's time we
    told you

how babies are made."

"OK," we said.

"Girl babies are made from sugar and spice
and all things nice," said mum.

"Boy babies are made from slugs and snails
and puppy dogs' tails,"
said dad.

"Some babies are delivered by dinosaurs."

"You can make them out of gingerbread," said mum.

"Sometimes you just find them under stones," said dad.

"You can grow them from seeds in po

"...the greenhouse," said mum.

"Or just squidge them out of tubes."

"Mummy laid an egg on the sofa," said dad.

"It …

... exploded.

And you shot out."

"Hee hee hee, ha ha ha, hoo hoo hoo. What a load of rubbish," we laughed.
"But you were nearly right about the SEEDS, the TUBE and the EGG."

"We don't think you know how babies are really made. So we're doing some drawings to show you."

"Mummy does have eggs. They are inside her tummy."

"And daddy has seeds in seed pods outside his body."

This fit

"Daddy also has a tube.
The seeds from the pods
come out of it."

here

"The tube goes into
mummy's tummy through
a little hole. Then the seeds
swim inside using their tails."

"Here are some ways

mummies and daddies
fit together."

SPACE
HOPPER

"The winner gets the egg and it starts to grow into a very small baby."

"The baby gets bigger

Mummy gets fatter

"When it's ready,
        out pops the baby."

"So now YOU know...

...and so does everyone else!"

First published in 1993 by
Jonathan Cape Ltd, 20 Vauxhall Bridge Road, London SW1V 2SA

Babette Cole has asserted the right to be
identified as the author and illustrator of this work

A CIP catalogue record for this book is
available from the British Library

ISBN 0 224 03645 9

Typeset in Sassoon Primary by Ampersand
Printed and bound in Italy by New Interlitho S.p.a., Milan